What a Night!

Story by Carmel Reilly
Illustrations by Rob Mancini

Contents

Chapter 1

Let's Go

"Are you ready?" asked Dad.

"I have my coat and hat, and the tickets for the show," said Kayla.

"And I've got the flowers for Mom," said Joe.

"Fantastic," said Dad. "Let's go."

Kayla, Joe, and Dad walked outside to the car. They were on their way to the Grand Theater in the city. Mom was already at the theater. She was performing in a musical there and tonight was the opening night.

"I can't wait to see Mom on the stage," said Joe, as they climbed into the car.

"It's going to be brilliant," said Kayla.

Dad tried to start the car, but nothing happened. He tried again and again.

"There's something wrong with the car," he said, "and now it's too late to call someone to fix it."

"How will we get into the city?" asked Kayla.

"Why don't we catch the train?" suggested Joe.

"The train is quick," said Dad, "but it's a long walk to the station."

"We could ask Emma to give us a ride," said Kayla. Emma was their next door neighbor.

"Great idea!" said Dad.

Chapter 2

On the Train

Emma drove Kayla, Joe, and Dad to the train station. They had just enough time to get tickets and wave goodbye to Emma before the train arrived.

"The trip should take about half an hour," said Dad.

After a few minutes, the train stopped at a station and there was an announcement.

"This train line is now closed, due to an accident," said a voice from the loudspeaker.

"Buses are waiting outside to take you from here to the city."

"That's not good news," said Dad. "The bus is going to be slow, because there is always so much traffic at this time of the night."

Chapter 3

On the Bus

"What if we don't get to the theater on time?" asked Kayla, as they boarded the bus. "Mom said that they close the doors just before the show starts. If we're late, we'll be locked out!"

Dad checked his watch. “I think we still have enough time to get there,” he said.

“As long as the bus doesn’t break down,” said Joe, looking worried.

After they had traveled for a few minutes, the bus turned onto the main road leading into the city center.

"Look!" said Joe. "I can see the Big Tower up ahead."

Dad peered out the window.

"The Big Tower is close to the Grand Theater," said Dad. "That means we don't have too far to go now."

Just then, the bus turned left into another street.

"What's happening?" asked Kayla. "We're going in a different direction!"

A woman sitting in front of Kayla turned around.

"The bus is going around the edge of the city center to pick up more people," she said. "It will take another fifteen minutes to get to the Central Bus Station."

"Another fifteen minutes!" Dad groaned. "That's too long."

"What if we walked from here?" asked Kayla.

"It would still take fifteen minutes to walk," said Dad.

"Maybe we could get a taxi?" said Kayla.

"Or we could take that!" exclaimed Joe. He pointed out the window to the other side of the street.

Chapter 4

A Different Way to Travel

Across the road from the bus was a horse and carriage. It had a large "For hire" sign on the side.

"I'd love to go to the theater in a horse and carriage," said Kayla, giggling.

"Let's see if it can take us to the theater then," said Dad. "The show will start soon, and it's our best chance of getting there on time."

As soon as the bus stopped, they got off quickly and hurried across the pedestrian crossing to the other side of the street.

FOR HIRE

The carriage driver smiled at them as they walked towards her.

"Where do you want to go?" she asked.

"Can you take us to the Grand Theater?" said Dad.

"Yes, I can," said the woman. "Are you going to see a show?"

"We're going to see a very special show," said Dad.

"Our mom is performing, and we need to get there in ten minutes," added Kayla.

"Well, in that case, I'll ask the horses to hurry up," the woman replied, laughing. "Climb on board."

Soon, Dad, Kayla, and Joe were all in the carriage.

"Off we go," the driver called, and the horses started to move forward.

After they had traveled for a few minutes, they started to slow down.

"It looks like there's a lot of traffic ahead," said the driver.

The carriage stopped moving.

"Perhaps we should walk from here," said Dad.

The driver shook her head. "Just wait a moment.
I think the traffic will start to move again very soon."

Chapter 5

A Shorter Way

The driver was right. After a short time, the traffic began to move.

"I know a shorter way to the theater," said the driver, as she steered the carriage into a side street.

"This will take us to the back of the Grand Theater. It's a lot faster than driving all the way around to the front."

It only took a few more minutes to get to the theater.

"Thank you so much," said Dad, as he paid the driver.

"I'm really glad I got you here on time!" she replied.

Kayla, Joe, and Dad raced along the side of the theater to the front entrance. They hurried inside and went to find their seats.

"What a trip!" said Dad.

"I'm so relieved that we got here on time!" said Kayla.

"That was fun. I've never taken so many different kinds of transportation before," said Joe.

Dad took the children's coats and hats and sat down.

"I feel really exhausted after all that rushing around," he said.

"You can relax now, Dad, and watch the show," said Kayla, as the lights began to dim.

As the lights came on for the intermission, Kayla turned to speak to Dad.

"Mom was amazing, wasn't she?" she said.

But Dad didn't reply. He was fast asleep under the pile of coats!